The Secret Mermaid

Penguin Peril

Sue Mongredien

Illustrated by Maria Pearson

For Holly Powell, with lots of love

First published in the UK in 2010 by Usborne Publishing Ltd., Usborne House,
83-85 Saffron Hill, London EC1N 8RT, England. www.usborne.com

A CIP catalogue record for this book is available from the British Library.

JF AMJJASOND/10 96096

ISBN 9781409506348

Printed in Reading, Berkshire, UK.

Contents

Shanti

Molly

Eloise

Leila

Undersea Kingdom

Queen Luna

Aisha

Iona

Phoebe

Chapter One

"There we go, that should do it," Mr. Holmes said, shoving another log onto the fire which blazed in the old stone hearth. Flames licked it hungrily, scorching its side and blackening the wood. Grey ribbons of smoke curled and twisted up into the chimney.

Molly Holmes watched dreamily, her eyes transfixed by the flickering amber lights of the flames as they danced over the logs. It was late in the afternoon and Dad had come back from work early, for a nice change. "A storm's on the way," he'd said, shivering as he closed the door behind him. "The boss said we should all get home while we could."

"Here, Molls, have one of these," her mum said at that moment, passing her a hot buttered crumpet on a plate. "This is what winter in the cottage is all about, right?"

Molly smiled as she bit into the crumpet and melted butter oozed deliciously into her mouth. "Mmmmm." She sighed happily. If this was what winter was going to be like in Gran's seaside cottage, she was going to enjoy the next few months very much, she decided.

This time last year, she, Mum and Dad had been in their old home, an ordinary modern house in a busy street. It had been a nice house, but it didn't have a proper fireplace, or the sloping ceilings and old-fashioned latched windows that Gran's cottage had. How cosy it was to sit in front of a blazing fire and warm your feet, Molly thought, wriggling her toes in their grey school tights. Much better than any radiator in her old house!

A lot of things had changed this year. Baby Toby had been born in January, and then they'd moved to live at the seaside with Gran in the summer. Best of all, Molly had discovered that, with the help of an enchanted shell, she was the new secret mermaid, often transforming magically into a mermaid at night, and enjoying the most wonderfully exciting underwater adventures!

Molly smiled to herself, thinking of her mermaid friends – then almost choked on her crumpet as she spotted something through the window. "Snow!" she yelled through her mouthful. "It's snowing!"

She jumped to her feet and raced over for a better look. Sure enough, down fell a whirling blizzard of white, the flakes flurrying and spinning through the darkening sky. Gran came to join her at the window, leaning on her stick.

"I hope it settles," she said with a smile. "The beach looks a different place when it's covered in snow. Utterly magical."

Molly stared out in wonder, feeling hypnotized by the dancing snowflakes. "What about the rock pools? Do they freeze?" she asked after a minute. She'd found something very strange in a rock pool just a few days earlier, which had led her into a brand-new mermaid quest. Molly had found it hard to think about anything else ever since. "Will the *sea* freeze?"

Gran put an arm around her. "The rock pools might freeze over, yes," she said. "But the sea won't freeze here. It's not still enough, is it? Think of the tide, forever churning and crashing."

"More to the point, it's not cold enough where we are," Dad said, as he clipped a metal fireguard to the wall. "At the north and south pole, though, where it's much colder, the water does freeze – or rather, lots of it already *has* frozen into huge ice shelves." He stood up and warmed his hands in front of the bright flames, then grinned at Molly. "Brrrr. I'm glad I'm not a polar bear or a penguin, aren't you? Just imagine how icy-cold they get, living there."

Molly smiled, deliberately not catching Gran's eye. For she'd already swum in frozen seas before, of course, back when she'd helped a mermaid called Shivana escape from an icy prison. She wasn't about to tell Dad that, though! Being the secret mermaid meant she wasn't allowed to discuss her adventures with *anybody*, not even Gran, who'd been the secret mermaid herself once upon a time.

Dad's words came back to Molly – about how he was glad he wasn't a polar bear or penguin – and a chill crept over her. She'd been called back to the Undersea Kingdom by the Merqueen recently because six different species – the seahorses, dolphins, penguins, whales, octopuses and turtles – had completely vanished from the oceans. Molly had vowed to help the Animal-Keeper mermaids, who each looked after a certain type of creature, to find them again, but so far it was proving very difficult. Not only had someone (or some*thing*) used dark magic to shrink the creatures to tiny sizes, making it almost impossible to track them down, but hostile monsters made from sand and rock had been guarding the missing creatures she'd found so far, which made the whole mission a lot more scary. Molly and her mermaid friends had been able to recover the missing seahorses and dolphins, and had managed to escape from the monsters each time, but she was already dreading meeting one of them again.

"Molly, come away from the window now, you're shivering," her mum said then, and Molly obeyed, even though she knew it wasn't just the cold that was making her shiver. It was the thought of a sandy hand stretching towards her, trying to clutch her in its strong, cold grip...

She sat by the fire again hurriedly, trying to shake the image out of her mind.

That night, Molly settled down in bed, pulling the covers up high around her ears as she heard the wind battering the roof and chimney outside. She imagined snow falling soft as feathers onto the beach and hoped it was settling on the rocks and sand, like a delicate white blanket. Then, as she rolled over sleepily, she caught sight of her special shell necklace which she always kept on her bedside table. On the necklace was strung a creamy-pink piece of shell, as well as a silver animal charm she'd been given by a friendly walrus. As she looked at it now, the shell started to glow, pulsing with pink and golden sparkles, twinkling with the promise of mermaid magic...

Molly shut her eyes quickly and a familiar tingling sensation went through her body. Then she felt as if she were dropping from a huge height – down, down, down. Moments later, she opened her eyes to find herself at the bottom of the ocean, with soft white sand below her and a tangle of coppery-brown seaweed billowing nearby. The water was cold and clear, and a couple of surprised-looking silver-grey cod were

staring at her with huge round eyes.

"Whoa! Where did you just swim from?" one asked, blinking.

"You are *fast*, girl. We didn't even see you coming!" the other marvelled.

Molly beamed. "It's magic," she told them happily, flipping her beautiful green mermaid tail and turning a somersault in the water. Oh, she just loved being a mermaid!

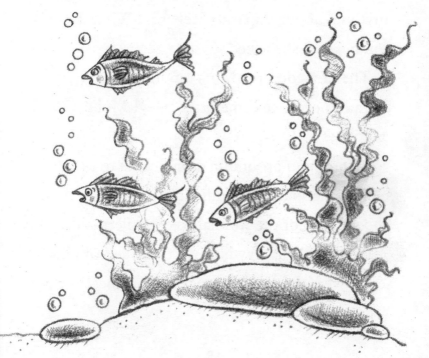

"Magic?" the first fish echoed. "Aha. So you're the one who made that weird sparkly iceberg, are you?"

"Oh yes, the terns can't talk about anything else right now," the second put in. "The way they keep chattering on and on about it… goodness! It's enough to give you earache."

Molly frowned, not understanding. She knew that a tern was a kind of bird, but didn't know anything about a sparkly iceberg. "What do you mean?" she asked.

The first cod opened its mouth to reply, but another voice came first. "Hey! Molly, is that you?"

Molly spun around in a semicircle to see a smiling mermaid swimming towards her. It was Phoebe, one of the Animal-Keeper mermaids. She had brown wavy hair with a circlet of pink sea-flowers threaded through it, and she wore a

green top with a sea-flower trim. Her tail was
bright pink.

"Hi, Phoebe," Molly said, remembering
that Phoebe was the mermaid who looked after
all the penguins. "How are things? Any news?"

Phoebe shook her head sadly as she drew
level with Molly. "Not really," she said.

"I feel as if I've searched every crevice of ice in the whole of Antarctica, looking for my penguins, and I've still found nothing. I don't know where else to try."

Molly glanced back at the fish. "These guys were just telling me about a strange sparkling iceberg the terns have seen," she said. "Do you know anything about that?"

"A sparkling iceberg?" Phoebe shook her head, looking interested. "First I've heard of it," she said. "Where is it?"

The fish gave Phoebe directions and then swam off with a friendly wave of their fins. Phoebe turned to Molly, looking excited. "Sounds to me as if there could be something magical about this iceberg," she said. "Let's investigate!"

Chapter Two

The two mermaids set off through the clear blue waters of the Antarctic, swerving around the huge looming glaciers and smaller drifting icebergs. The sea still seemed so empty without the whales, turtles and octopuses, Molly thought sadly, although she was cheered to see a pod of hourglass dolphins swimming along together at one point. They didn't look quite right, though, she thought, watching them with a frown.

Dolphins were usually always so energetic
and bouncy – but these ones seemed slow and
subdued.

She mentioned her worries to Phoebe as
they swam, and Phoebe nodded. "You're
right," she said. "And Aisha is quite concerned.

The dolphins seem to have lost their speed –
none of them can swim so fast any more. It's
really important for dolphins to be able to race
away from sharks and other predators to avoid
being attacked. We're hoping they'll recover
soon but they're not quite back to full strength
just yet." She looked sad. "The seahorses aren't
quite back to normal yet either. They can't
camouflage themselves properly, not like
they used to."

Molly bit her lip. That didn't sound good. Before she could reply, though, Phoebe had stopped swimming suddenly and was pointing. "I think this is the iceberg the cod were talking about," she said. "But I can't see any sparkles, can you?"

Molly stared at the huge block of ice, white-blue and glistening as it hung in the water in front of them. She and Phoebe were still underwater, and the iceberg was so huge, it almost touched the seabed below them. "No," she said reluctantly. "Is this definitely the right iceberg?"

Phoebe nodded. "It should be. It's exactly where the fish said it would be," she said. "Come on, let's swim around it. Maybe we'll be able to see the sparkles from around the other side."

"Wait," Molly said, realizing something.

"The cod said that the *terns* had spotted the sparkles, didn't they? So they probably saw them from the air! Which means the sparkles must be right at the top of the iceberg."

25

"Yes, of course!" Phoebe cried. "Good thinking, Molly. Let's swim up to the surface and take a look from there."

Molly pushed herself up through the icy water until her head was in the air. Although it was the middle of the night for her, down here at the southernmost part of the world, there was daylight, and a pale yellow sun filtered dimly through filmy clouds. And oh, it was so cold! When she was a mermaid she never seemed to feel the cold in water, but being in the open air was a different matter. A freezing

wind blew against Molly's face,
making her teeth chatter together.

She stared up towards the
top of the iceberg and then
let out a gasp. "Oh, look!"
she said. "There *is*
something sparkling
up there!"

She and Phoebe tipped their heads back,
trying to get a better look at the iceberg's top,
but it was so high that they couldn't see very
much. Molly tried leaping out
of the water like a dolphin,
but couldn't get high
enough to see the
sparkles any better,
and merely landed
back in the sea
with a splash.

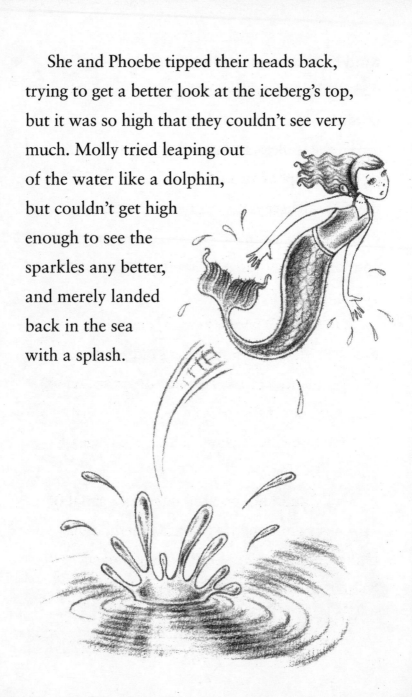

But yes, there was definitely a golden pulsing light flickering up there, they were both sure of that.

The two of them ducked below the surface again while they thought what to do. "We've got to find a way to get up there and have a proper look," Phoebe said. "What could it be, I wonder? It certainly looks magical, don't you think?"

"Definitely," Molly agreed, her mind racing. "Maybe there's some kind of an enchantment over the iceberg. But if so, what? And who put it there?"

"We know, we know!" came a chorus of voices just then.

Molly and Phoebe turned to see a shoal of sardines swimming up towards them, their bodies glinting silver-blue as they moved. "What do you mean?" Phoebe asked them.

"We saw, we saw!" the sardines chanted, swirling before the mermaids in a dizzying pattern. It was like seeing inside a silvery kaleidoscope, Molly thought, blinking.

"You saw what?" Phoebe asked patiently, winking at Molly. "Spit it out, guys."

"Scary mermaid, scary mermaid," the sardines answered as one, their big round eyes solemn and staring as they circled and spun.

"Scary mermaid? What do you mean?"
Phoebe asked. "What did she look like?"

The sardines all spoke at once, and this time,
they each called out different things.

"Black cape!"

"Hooked nose!"

"Evil smile!"

"Angry eyes!"

Molly felt faint at the words. She exchanged glances with Phoebe, who looked pale and scared too. "Surely they don't mean…" Molly began.

Phoebe had a tight, grim look on her face. "It must be Carlotta," she said. "She's back."

Molly's head was reeling. This was truly awful news – just what she and the other mermaids had been dreading. Carlotta was a bad mermaid, known as the Dark Queen, who'd previously tried to seize control of the oceans by enslaving all sorts of animals and stealing the pieces of a magic conch shell, looked after by the Shell-Keeper mermaids. But, with Molly's help, the mermaids and a whole host of sea creatures had fought together to defeat Carlotta, strip away her bad magic and banish her. Now it seemed she'd returned, though...and had found a way to use her magical powers once again.

Phoebe groaned. "The Merqueen suspected that Carlotta might have something to do with the missing animals," she said. "But why has she been taking them all? Some kind of punishment for the way they helped the Shell-Keepers, do you think?"

"Maybe," Molly replied, speaking in a low voice. "She did look really furious when we caught her and sent her away. This could be her revenge." She shivered at the thought.

Phoebe sighed. "Well, whatever she's up to, she's been here to the Antarctic and cast some kind of magic over this iceberg and…" She brightened as an idea struck her. "Maybe she's hidden some of the creatures in the ice," she suggested, the words tumbling out in her haste. "Eloise and Aisha told me how tiny their seahorses and dolphins were when you found them. What if Carlotta's done the same with some other creatures and they're trapped in this iceberg? Most of my penguins live in icy waters – and so do many of the whales. They could all be in here!"

Chapter Three

"I bet you're right," Molly said, her spirits
rising. Carlotta might be cunning, but the
mermaids had beaten her before. Who was to
say they couldn't do the same again?

"Come on," Phoebe said, swimming back
up to the surface again. Molly followed,
watching as her friend stretched out of the
water, trying to get a handhold on the icy wall
to pull herself up. Her fingers scrabbled

uselessly against it, though, and she slipped back in.

"Maybe I can hoist you up?" Molly wondered. "Or perhaps you could perch on one of my shoulders?"

"We'll have to be quick," Phoebe said doubtfully. "We won't be able to breathe out of the water for very long." She shrugged. "I can't think of anything else though. Let's try it."

The two mermaids arranged themselves so that Phoebe was balanced on Molly's right shoulder, then Molly pushed up out of the water as high as she could. "Oh, I still can't really see it properly," Phoebe sighed, sliding off Molly and back into the water. She frowned. "Who could help us, I wonder?"

Molly tried to think of all the sea creatures she'd met who might be able to pull themselves up such a huge block of ice. Lobsters were good climbers, she knew, but they didn't live in such cold waters, so there wouldn't be any around here. Who else?

Then she laughed. "We've missed the most obvious answer," she said. "We can ask a bird – one of the terns, maybe – to fly down and look closely at the sparkly ice for us."

Phoebe clapped her hands together. "Of course," she said. "Why didn't I think of that? It's lucky you're here, Molly!" She put two fingers in her mouth and gave a piercing whistle.

They waited a few moments and then,
swooping through the air, came one of
the most graceful-looking birds Molly had ever
seen. It had long, narrow wings, mostly white
with black tips, as if it had dipped them in paint
pots. She held her breath as the bird glided
down towards them. It was enormous, way
bigger than any gull she'd seen before. Surely
this wasn't a tern? She'd thought they were
quite small birds.

"It's an albatross," Phoebe said in a low voice to Molly, then she smiled and waved at the bird as it hung hovering in the air before them. "Hi," she said. "Small favour to ask. Would you mind checking out this iceberg for us? There's something sparkling at the top of it and we want to know what it is."

The albatross blinked at them with small round eyes, and then let out a honk of surprise as it noticed Molly's necklace. "Oh my!" it exclaimed. "Is that the animal charm? You bet I'll help you, then. I'll be right back."

Molly touched the silvery disc she wore on her special shell necklace and smiled. A walrus had given it to her back in the summer after Molly had helped free the creatures Carlotta had enslaved. The walrus had promised that if she were ever in trouble, sea creatures everywhere would come to her assistance. So far, this was proving to be true...and the charm also seemed to have some other special powers, as Molly had been finding out. "Thank you," she shouted after the albatross as it flapped its mighty wings and flew effortlessly to the top of the iceberg.

"Okaaaay," they heard the albatross say. "So what have we here?" He had perched on the edge of the ice, and the mermaids watched anxiously as he peered at it closely. "Whoa!" he exclaimed. "No way!"

"What do you see?" Phoebe shouted up.
"What is it?"

The albatross swooped back down to
them, looking puzzled. "Weird," it said,
shaking its head. "There's an air bubble
beneath the ice and it's full of thousands – no,
millions – of tiny – and I do mean tiny –
little… Well, they looked like *birds*."
It frowned, clicking its
beak. "Tiny little birds
in an iceberg. But how
can that be?"

"Oh my goodness!"
Phoebe cried, her
eyes sparkling
with happiness.
"The penguins!
We've found
the penguins!"

"Thank you, thank you," Molly said to the albatross. "That's wonderful news." She quickly explained what had happened to the dolphins and seahorses, and how they knew now that Carlotta was involved in their disappearances.

"Oh my!" the albatross squawked in alarm. "So you need to get those penguins free, right? Want me to have a try?"

Phoebe smiled. "Yes, please!" she said. "That would be wonderful."

The albatross soared back up into the air and to the top of the huge iceberg. Then the two mermaids heard it tapping on the ice with its beak, softly at first, and then harder... followed by a cross-sounding honk.

At last the albatross flew back down, looking defeated. "Sorry, ladies," it said, swooping to land on the water and tucking its wings by its sides. "The ice is totally solid up there. My beak's pretty tough but it's not *that* tough. I couldn't even make a dent in it."

Molly felt her spirits sink, but tried not to show her disappointment. "No worries," she said. "Thanks for trying all the same."

The albatross gave a little shrug. "Good luck," he said. "If I can do anything else, just holler."

"Thanks, we will," Molly replied, watching the albatross flap up into the air once more and glide away. She turned towards Phoebe as they both slid back below the surface. "Well, at least we know where the penguins *are*," she said. "And that the Dark Queen hid them there. And…" Then a terrible thought struck her as she remembered the horrible monsters that had been guarding the seahorses and dolphins. Would there be another one around here, watching over the penguins? A shiver ran down her back.

Maybe it was spying on them right now!

"We need to get the penguins out of there as soon as possible," she said, feeling herself fill with determination. "But it'll be difficult if we can't even reach the bit of the iceberg where they are. Unless... unless we could *move* the iceberg somehow – turn it on its side? Then we'd be able to reach the penguins."

Phoebe bit her lip. "Nice idea, Molly, but how are we ever going to move this beast? It must weigh an absolute ton."

"Maybe if we tie seaweed ropes around it, we can ask the whales to help us heave it over…" Molly began. Then she sighed as she remembered that the whales were still missing, presumably tiny themselves and hidden away in a remote part of the ocean. "I miss the whales," she said sadly.

"I miss the penguins," Phoebe added, and slapped the side of the iceberg in frustration. "Oh! What can we do?"

"You could try going *inside* the iceberg," came a shy little voice from beneath them.

Chapter Four

Phoebe and Molly both looked around, but couldn't see the speaker. The voice had sounded very faint, as if it were some distance away. "Who said that?" Phoebe asked. "Where are you?"

"I'm down here," came the sweet voice again. "Under the iceberg. There's a big crack in the ice – come and see."

Molly dived down immediately all the way to the bottom of the iceberg, which was just a metre or so above the seabed. Perched on a rock was a pretty yellow starfish, which waved one of its spiny arms. "Hi," said the starfish. "There, look. See the hole? You might not be able to climb up the outside of the iceberg, but perhaps you could clamber up inside it, and reach the penguins that way?"

Molly and Phoebe looked at each other. "It's worth a try," Phoebe decided. "Icebergs often have big cracks inside that are made when they're forming. Thank you, starfish!"

The starfish blushed a pinky-red. "You're welcome," it said, sounding pleased. "Good luck!"

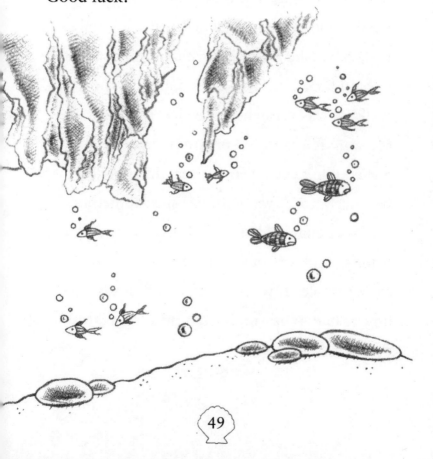

Phoebe and Molly peered inside the crack, which split the base of the iceberg, stretching up inside it like a long, icy tunnel. "Brilliant," Phoebe said. "Come on, Molly, let's see how far we can get."

She slithered into the crack and began pushing her way along the tunnel. It wasn't really wide enough to swim properly, Molly realized as she followed, which meant she had to haul herself up using her hands on the icy walls. It was eerie inside the iceberg, with only the sound of her own breathing in her ears. She couldn't even hear the sea any more. It was dark, too, even with her special mermaid eyes that enabled her to see through midnight waters. And, of course, it was absolutely freezing cold. It wasn't long before Molly's fingers had gone numb from pushing against the wall.

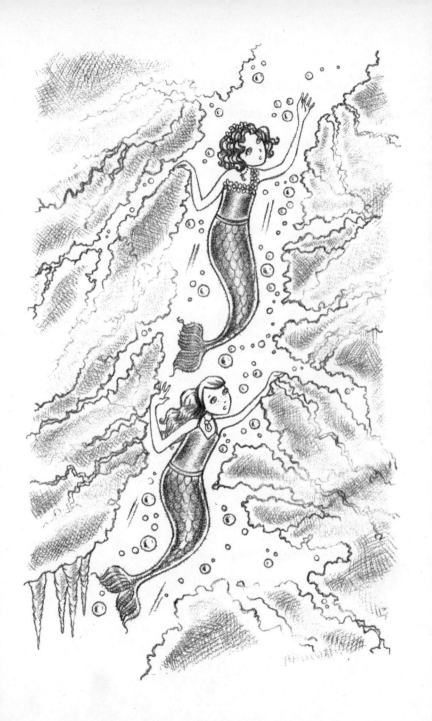

Phoebe was ahead of her, and after just a few minutes, Molly could see that Phoebe's whole body was shaking violently with the cold. Molly's arms were covered in goosebumps too and her teeth were chattering so hard she couldn't stop them. The cold was making her head ache, and her fingers felt numb.

She found herself wishing she was back at home, curled up in front of the roaring log fire with a plate of hot buttery crumpets again... How much colder was it going to *get* in this iceberg, anyway?

Molly could feel herself becoming weaker and weaker. Her bones ached with the freezing temperature, and the muscles in her arms were tired from dragging herself along. She wasn't sure how much longer she could go on – but she knew that she had to help Phoebe, had to keep up with her friend, if they were to stand a chance of rescuing the poor trapped penguins.

The tunnel opened up into a sort of chamber, an icy cave full of freezing water. Phoebe stopped still suddenly and turned around to face Molly, her arms clutched around herself, and her teeth chattering. "I'm s-s-sorry," she said, barely able to speak for shivering. "I can't d-d-do this. I'm just too c-c-c-cold. I think we should go b-b-back."

Molly's first feeling was that of relief – thank goodness they could get out of this miserable place! Phoebe looked every bit as numb and defeated as she'd been feeling herself, and Molly hugged her, hoping they could warm each other up a little. Then she remembered the penguins and felt guilty about abandoning the climb. "But w-w-w-what are w-w-w-we going to d-d-d-do, then?" she asked, pulling apart from Phoebe again. "I c-c-can't think of any other w-w-way of getting near the penguins."

There was a miserable silence for a moment, then Molly added, "I d-d-d-don't know how the penguins manage it, living at the S-S-S-South Pole. I wish I could keep out the c-c-cold like they d-d-do."

No sooner had she said the words than she felt a sudden warmth flooding through her veins, filling her whole body, right down to each

fingertip. She gasped in
surprise and then
noticed that the
animal charm
around her neck
was glowing
brightly. A hologram
of a penguin figure
appeared on its silver
surface, glittering magically
with rainbow colours. The charm's magic had
worked again!

"Oh my goodness!" she cried. "I'm warm –
this charm has made me warm!" She put a hand
to Phoebe's face, and Phoebe jumped at the heat
from her fingers.

"Wow!" said Phoebe, now warming her own
hands on Molly's, as if Molly were a hot-water
bottle. "That is a-a-a-amazing!"

Molly grinned. "I know," she said. "I can't believe it. I actually can't feel the cold at all now." It was true. It was as if her blood had thickened, or she'd grown an extra skin that protected her from the icy temperature. "Let me carry on alone to see if I can find the penguins," she said. "You go back into the sea and get warm again."

"Are you sh-sh-sure?" Phoebe asked, still shivering. "I hate to l-l-l-leave you on your own, but…"

"Honestly, I'm fine," Molly repeated. "You get out of here before you freeze solid. I'll see how far up I can go."

Phoebe vanished back down the icy tunnel, and Molly pushed on, swimming higher through the icy water inside the iceberg. She felt as warm as toast now. How amazing – she'd wished to be able to keep warm like a penguin and the animal charm seemed to have granted her wish! This was the third time it had happened – that she'd wished to have an ability of a particular animal, and the charm had magically given it to her. She'd been able to camouflage herself like a seahorse, swim extra-fast like a dolphin, and now keep warm like a penguin. How cool was that? She smiled to herself. How *warm*, rather...

The tunnel narrowed suddenly and came to a dead end, and Molly's optimism vanished. Oh no! Was this as far as she could go? She would have to turn back, it seemed, without reaching the penguins. She must have swum a long way up the iceberg too – surely she had to be nearly at the top? What bad luck that she couldn't quite make it all the way.

But wait...something was happening. The ice in front of her was creaking...cracking...

and suddenly it was moving.
Molly gave a scream of fright
as a huge, icy claw shot out
from the end of the tunnel –
and then an icy face emerged,
its yellow eyes staring at
her, and its mouth twisted
in a smile.

Molly flinched as the
creature's claw – or was it
a foot? – made a swiping
movement towards her and she
darted back down the tunnel, her heart
pounding. What *was* this thing? She'd
never heard of a creature that lived in ice like
this. Unless it was something magicked up by
the Dark Queen to guard the penguins, just
like the sand and rock monsters had been
watching over the seahorses and dolphins!

The ice-monster – if that was what it was –
was moving faster now, coming after Molly
through the tunnel, making a horrible clattering,
scraping sound as it went. Back plunged Molly
into the icy chamber, with the monster

following, its eyes glittering as it watched her.
It was like a huge, icy spider, with eight long
legs which ended in sharp points, coming from
a fat, round icy body, glistening white. Its head
was on top of its body, and Molly could see

horribly pointed fangs coming from its mouth – fangs that would surely make quick work of a mere mermaid. Terror rushed through her. What was she going to do?

She thought hard, her skin prickling all over with fear. She had to get past the ice monster somehow, or she'd have no chance of reaching the penguins. She couldn't just slink back to Phoebe without putting up some kind of fight!

The monster swiped one of its front legs towards her, the pointed end looking as sharp as a knife as it whistled past, and Molly was so frightened that she barely had the breath to scream. What was she going to *do*?

Molly pressed herself back against the icy wall of the chamber. Suddenly the ice gave

way behind her,
melted by the
warmth of her
body, and she
fell through
into another
crack in the
iceberg. The
monster hissed
and scuttled
after her.

"Go away,"
Molly whimpered,
scrambling further up
into this new crack,
expecting that at any minute
the ice-creature would lunge at her. Would it
take her to the Dark Queen as a prisoner?
Would it hurt her?

Oh, why had she ever thought this was a good idea? Why had she trusted the starfish? Maybe the starfish had been told by the Dark Queen to send the mermaids up there! Maybe the whole thing was a trick!

Chapter Five

The monster was closing in on her now, its eyes cold, its front legs waving threateningly. Molly scrambled frantically up the tunnel away from it, trying desperately to think of a way to fight it. It was so big, and she was just so scared – surely it was impossible?

Her animal charm felt hot against her skin and suddenly an idea popped into her head. Maybe she could use her charm to *melt* the ice-monster?

"Stay back!" she yelled at the creature, fumbling to unfasten her necklace from around her throat. She dangled it in the water between them, trying not to tremble as the monster scuttled closer, making a sickening chomping sound with its fangs.

The monster lashed out again with one of its icy front legs and Molly seized the moment to swish her necklace through the water at it in defence.

There was a sizzling sound as the charm struck the monster's leg…and then the monster let out a shriek of rage as the end of this leg was melted clean away. Hope surged within Molly,

but a second later the monster reared up on its hind legs and rushed blindly at her. It was angry now – and out for revenge.

Molly's heart was pounding but she somehow managed to swish her necklace through the water at the monster again. The silver animal charm hit the creature right between the eyes this time, and the monster gave another screech as the front part of its head collapsed, melting to water from the heat of Molly's charm.

Its legs buckled beneath it and the monster sank to its knees. Had she beaten it? Was the fight over?

No. With one last burst of effort the monster swung a leg in Molly's direction, but luckily Molly managed to use her charm to whack the monster smartly on its leg, and that too melted and was gone.

Molly held her breath but the ice-monster – or rather the remains of it – was quite still now. Relief throbbed through her and she felt dizzy suddenly, overcome with exhaustion now that it was all over. Thank goodness for her charm! It had saved her again – and this time from the scariest monster yet.

Shakily, she put her necklace back on, still breathing heavily. She had defeated the horrible creature – now she just had to get up to the penguins as fast as she could, in case there was another monster lurking somewhere in the iceberg.

Quickly, she swam up through the tunnel, which led into another large crack in the iceberg. And – oh! All of a sudden she was out in the open air with no water to breathe in any more! She gazed around quickly, trying to work out which way to go. Where were the penguins?

She was completely disoriented.

Taking shallow breaths of air, she scrambled up a small icy ridge, pulling herself to the very top of the iceberg. Her muscles were burning with tiredness now as she hauled her body up, her tail useless and cumbersome out of the water. But yes...there were the bright golden sparkles shining just in front of her! She slithered quickly towards them, heaving herself along with her hands.

A tight pinching band of pain was starting to form around her head. She really needed to get back in the water, fast, so that she could breathe again with her mermaid gills. But there was the air bubble just as the albatross had said – half full with water, and packed with millions of tiny black-and-white birds. The ice had been too solid to break with the albatross's beak, but maybe she'd be able to melt it...

Trying to ignore her dizziness, Molly got straight to work, pressing her still-hot animal charm around the frozen edges of the bubble. The thick ice melted to water with the heat of the metal and, before long, there was a faint hissing sound of escaping air. She'd broken through to the air bubble!

Quickly Molly picked at the melting ice with her fingers, making the hole in it larger and larger, and then, all of a sudden... whoosh! Before her eyes, the tiny penguins began streaming out of the bubble, growing bigger and bigger as they left it behind, whizzing down the glacier on their bellies as it if were an enormous icy slide!

"Wheeeee!" they squealed, as they plopped one by one into the water below. Phoebe was waiting there, her face a picture of joy as she greeted them all, hugging them to her in happiness and relief. "Oh, hello! You're back, oh, it's so lovely to see you again!" she cried again and again.

By the time the last penguin had escaped, Molly's chest felt tight, and black spots danced

before her eyes. She flung herself over the
edge of the glacier, sliding down it on
her tail and screaming hoarsely as
she whizzed down the almost
vertical drop like the penguins
had done, all the way into
the sea. And then…oh,
the relief of getting
her breath back!

Phoebe hugged her with grateful tears in her eyes. "Molly, well done! You did it!"

"*We* did it," Molly corrected her, smiling at the sight of all the penguins diving gracefully through the sea, their black-and-white feathers so sharp and clean in the water, like smart little suits.

But then she noticed that some of the penguins were shivering unhappily. "We're so c-c-c-cold," one of them said, wrapping its glossy wings around its body and trembling.

"It's really f-f-f-freezing here," another agreed.

Phoebe stared in surprise. "But...it always *is* cold in the Antarctic," she said. She thought for a moment, frowning. "Maybe it's because you've been trapped in that iceberg for so long. You probably need to huddle together a bit, like you do on land. I'm sure you'll warm up soon."

Molly bit her lip, not feeling so certain. She remembered how the dolphins had swum slower than usual since they'd been captured, and apparently the seahorses no longer had their camouflaging powers. Being shrunk and trapped seemed to mean that the creatures had lost their special abilities – had the Dark Queen done this to deliberately weaken them? Or maybe...

A terrible thought struck Molly and she clutched at her animal charm, which was now cooler. "Phoebe – I've just thought," she gulped. "Since I've had this charm, I've been able to wish for special powers: keeping warm like a penguin, swimming at super-speed like a dolphin and camouflaging myself like a seahorse. What if...?" She could hardly bear to say the words. "What if it's *me* who's stripping the animals of their powers somehow, with my charm?"

Phoebe hesitated, then shook her head. "No – I'm sure it can't be you." She leaned over and peered at the animal charm. "I've never seen another one of these, but I've heard about one, in the old mermaid stories, which could lend its owner animal abilities in times of need. It sounds as if you've got that very charm now – what an amazing gift!"

"But—" Molly began. She'd been about to say it seemed too much of a coincidence that she could do all these special things just as the creatures themselves had lost those very powers – but just then she felt a tugging sensation all over, which always marked the end of her mermaid adventures.

"Oh, no," she groaned. "I'll have to go soon."

Phoebe threw her arms around her. "Thanks again, Molly," she said. "For everything. And don't worry, I'm sure the penguins will be fine.

I've just got to get them all back in their homes now and settled, and…"

But the rest of her sentence was lost, for a strong current was dragging Molly away. Bubbles swirled all around her body and she was pulled higher and higher towards the light.

Molly opened her eyes with a start, her heart racing. She was back in her bed and…she blinked, feeling confused. Something was different in her bedroom, she thought groggily. A strange, unfamiliar light was gleaming through the curtains and it took her a moment to realize what was causing it.

Snow! Had it settled? She leaped out of bed, barely noticing how cold it was up in her attic room, and rushed over to the window to investigate. "Oh!" she cried, as she pulled the curtain aside. For snow was still falling in big white flakes, soft and silent, spinning through the air. Her eyes widened as she saw that the beach was completely covered in a layer of it, the rock pools invisible beneath their cold white coating, the sand and seagrass and rocks of the bay all hidden from view. "Wow," she breathed, watching the waves rise and fall through the blizzard.

Her thoughts turned to the penguins and she wondered how they were coping. She knew that some penguins liked warmer waters anyway, but that lots of them lived at the South Pole, where it was bitterly cold all year round. She hoped they were managing to keep warm somehow, maybe by huddling together as Phoebe had suggested.

She shivered suddenly herself and went to put on her slippers and dressing gown. Then she smiled as she caught sight of her animal charm, back on her bedside table after last night's adventure. Somehow she didn't think it would keep her warm now she was out of the water! She pressed the animal charm against her face but it felt cool now, as if it were just an ordinary silver disc. "Thank you," she said under her breath. Now that the Dark Queen was back, and up to her evil tricks again, Molly knew that she and her mermaid friends would need every bit of magic they could get if they were to defeat her a second time.

She set her necklace down carefully again, then glanced out of the window at the sea. "I'll be back soon," she whispered. "I promise. And I'll do my very best to set all the animals free – so the Dark Queen had better watch out!"

The End

Read on for a sneak preview of Molly's next magical underwater adventure...

Turtle Trouble

Molly closed her eyes and immediately felt as if she were falling down a great hole. She knew that this was the mermaid magic at work, but it was still the strangest sensation – exhilarating and scary all at the same time. After a few moments, she could hear a rushing sound around her and knew, with a thrill of anticipation, that she was back in the ocean, and that she was a mermaid again, with her own beautiful green tail. Hurrah! She opened her eyes and blinked, staring around the watery world. Often she found herself in an unfamiliar place at the start of her mermaid adventures – somewhere far out in the ocean, sometimes in tropical seas, sometimes in freezing waters. This time... She smiled as she recognized the high, jewel-adorned ceiling above her head, and the glittering golden thrones across the grand underwater hall. This time, she knew exactly where she was – in the Merqueen's palace, right at the heart of the Undersea Kingdom! But why had she been brought here?

"My dear, it's good to have you back," came a voice, and Molly turned to see Queen Luna, the gracious mermaid queen, swimming towards her. The Merqueen was quite the most beautiful creature Molly had ever met, with her long chestnut-coloured hair twisted up elegantly on her head. Her eyes were wise, kind and understanding, and her voice was low and musical. Today, though, to Molly's dismay, the queen appeared grave and unhappy, her lovely face etched with lines of worry.

Molly opened her mouth to speak, then closed it again. She'd been about to ask if the queen was all right, but she wasn't sure that it was polite to ask a queen such a personal question. "Hello," she said instead, bobbing a neat curtsy.

The queen swam over and took her hands. "Thank you so much for your help with our sea creatures," she said, squeezing Molly's fingers gently. "We are all extremely grateful for your courage and quick-thinking in helping rescue so many of our animal friends. But there have been developments since you were last here. Come," she said, beckoning towards an open door.

"The Animal-Keeper mermaids are waiting for us in the courtyard."

Molly followed the Merqueen out through the arching doorway into the pretty courtyard garden at the centre of the palace. Exotic-looking emerald-green and rust-red sea-plants rippled in the gentle current, and the ground was laid with thousands of round, white pebbles that gleamed brightly in the light. In one corner of the garden was a huge pink scallop shell, with a cluster of large, smooth rocks around it, on which were sitting six other mermaids, all gazing expectantly at Molly and the Merqueen.

The mermaids were called Eloise, Shanti, Iona, Aisha, Phoebe and Leila, and they each looked after one of the groups of creatures that had recently vanished from the seas.

"Hi, guys," Molly said, smiling as she swam over to them.

"Hi, Molly," Phoebe and Aisha chorused, and the others smiled briefly, although they, too, seemed anxious.

Molly felt her insides turn over. Everybody seemed so solemn – had some other creatures gone missing now as well? What was going on?

To find out what happens next, read

The **Secret Mermaid**

Turtle Trouble

To find out more
about Molly and all her
mermaid friends, and have
some magical ocean fun,
check out
www.thesecretmermaid.co.uk

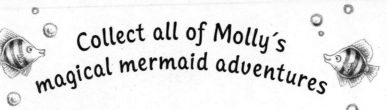

Collect all of Molly's magical mermaid adventures

Enchanted Shell ⊙ 9780746096154

Molly is transported to the Undersea Kingdom for the first time, where she discovers she is the secret mermaid!

Seaside Adventure ⊙ 9780746096161

To help Ella recover her piece of the magical conch, Molly must find a way to trap an angry killer whale.

Underwater Magic ⊙ 9780746096178

Can Molly find some pirate treasure to win back Delphi's shell from a grumpy sea urchin?

Reef Rescue ⊙ 9780746096192

Molly must help Coral find her shell to restore the ocean reefs, but a swarm of jellyfish stands in their way…

Deep Trouble ⊙ 9780746096185

Pearl's conch piece is trapped in an undersea volcano and guarded by sea snakes. How can she and Molly release it?

Return of the Dark Queen ⊙ 9780746096208

Molly must save Shivana from an Arctic prison before the Shell-Keeper mermaids can finally face the Dark Queen and complete the magical conch.

Seahorse SOS ⊙ 9781409506324

There's more trouble in the Undersea Kingdom and
Molly joins in the search for the missing seahorses.

Dolphin Danger ⊙ 9781409506331

Molly and Aisha can hear faint calls for help but the
dolphins are nowhere to be seen. Where can they be?

Penguin Peril ⊙ 9781409506348

Could the Dark Queen be behind the mysterious
disappearance of the penguins from the icy seas?

Turtle Trouble ⊙ 9781409506355

There are some scary monsters lurking in the coral reef and
they're guarding the turtles Molly has come to set free!

Whale Rescue ⊙ 9781409506393

Molly must not only save the trapped whales but also
her mermaid friend, Leila.

The Dark Queen's Revenge ⊙ 9781409506409

The Dark Queen is back and she wants to rule the
Undersea Kingdom with her bad magic. Can Molly put
an end to her vile plans?

For more enchanting adventures
log on to
www.fiction.usborne.com